SAMANTHA CARDIGAN

and the *Genie's Revenge*

INTERNATIONAL
ADVENTURERS

D1147707

DAVID SUTHERLAND   DAVID ROBERTS

For Jack
D.S.

For George and Lynne
D.R.

First published in Great Britain 2004
by Egmont Books Ltd
239 Kensington High Street, London W8 6SA
Text copyright © David Sutherland 2004
Illustrations copyright © David Roberts 2004
The author and illustrator have asserted their moral rights.
Paperback ISBN 1 4052 0297 1
10 9 8 7 6 5 4 3 2 1
A CIP catalogue record for this title is available from the British Library.
Printed in U.A.E.

Contents

Red Bananas

A Very Sore Toe

From the scorpion's point of view, Samantha Cardigan's shoe was just a shady place to hide. It didn't mean any harm. She had only taken off her trainers for a few minutes to stretch her toes.

She and Rabbit, International Adventurers, had been hiking all day under the hot desert sun. They still had seven miles to go to the oasis. Samantha Cardigan rubbed sun cream on Rabbit's ears, then she sat down and picked up her shoe.

'You know,' she said, waving
it about casually, 'that telegram
we got from the Sheikh doesn't
make any sense.'

She put the shoe down and took a piece
of paper from her pocket. She read it aloud:

Dear Miss Cardigan
please come
immediately.
Daughter stuck on
ceiling!
Yours gratefully,
Sheikh Ali

Samantha Cardigan frowned at the telegram. 'How can anyone get stuck on a ceiling?'

Rabbit shrugged. Without thinking, she crushed the telegram into a ball and tossed it over her shoulder. She picked up her shoe again and was about to put it on, when suddenly a thick cloud of smoke gushed up from the desert floor.

What's happened?

Samantha Cardigan was so startled
that she dropped her shoe and scuttled
away backwards. Rabbit ran around
behind her. The smoke cleared and an
enormous genie appeared.

'How dare you insult me!' he bellowed.
'I have been lord of these sands since
the beginning of time – and now you
come to throw rubbish in my face.'

Oops!

8

Samantha Cardigan knew it was
wrong to throw rubbish on the ground.
She picked up the ball of paper and
stuffed it back into her pocket.

'I'm really very sorry,' she pleaded.
'Honest . . . I won't do it again.'

'This carelessness shall not go unpunished. Give me your shoes,' cried the genie angrily.

'My shoes? What for?'

'That you may finish your journey barefoot. Perhaps then you will learn some respect for my great desert.'

Reluctantly, Samantha Cardigan handed the genie her trainers.

His body was huge, but his feet were tiny, so he tried on one of the shoes. He didn't know there was a scorpion inside. The scorpion only did what was natural.

Take that!

Howling like a madman, the genie danced about on one foot, clutching his swollen toe. Samantha Cardigan grabbed her trainers and ran off across the dunes with Rabbit.

The scorpion scurried away to find another home.

Owwww! My toe!

Zara, Balloon Girl

They walked all day, arriving at the oasis late in the afternoon. Tents were set up all around a watering hole. The Sheikh was easy to find, as his was the largest tent.

He welcomed Samantha Cardigan and Rabbit with a low bow, saying, 'We are greatly honoured! My home is your home, for as long as you wish to stay.'

Turning to his wife, he called something
in another language. She took a brass pot
from the fire and poured sweet mint
tea into three glasses.

Samantha Cardigan and Rabbit were grateful for the refreshing drink after a long, dry day. She took a packet of crisps from her bag and passed them around.

'I must say,' she commented, 'I didn't know what to make of your telegram.'

'I can well imagine,' said the Sheikh. 'More tea? No? Then come and see for yourselves.'

Get me down!

The Sheikh lifted the flap of his tent and they went inside. Everyone took off their shoes – except for Rabbit, of course, who didn't wear shoes. Samantha Cardigan looked up and there, floating on the ceiling, was a girl of about six years old.

'This is my darling daughter, Zara,' said the Sheikh. 'Yesterday after dinner, she simply floated up off the carpet. Imagine if it had happened outside – she would have blown away like a feather.'

Zara! Come back

Zara waved and tried to smile. Samantha Cardigan waved back. She had never seen anything like it.

'What do you make of this, Rabbit?' she asked.

Rabbit whispered something in her ear. She gave him an angry look.

'How can you be so selfish? No, you may not have a lettuce.'

Reaching into her backpack, Samantha Cardigan took out an inflatable stepladder and a coil of rope. She blew up the ladder and the Sheikh held it steady while she climbed up towards the young girl.

She tied the rope around Zara's ankle and carefully the Sheikh pulled his daughter down.

Then they took Zara outside and tied her to one of the tent pegs. Everyone stood looking up at the balloon girl, bobbing on the end of the rope.

'What do you think could have caused this strange condition?' Samantha Cardigan asked.

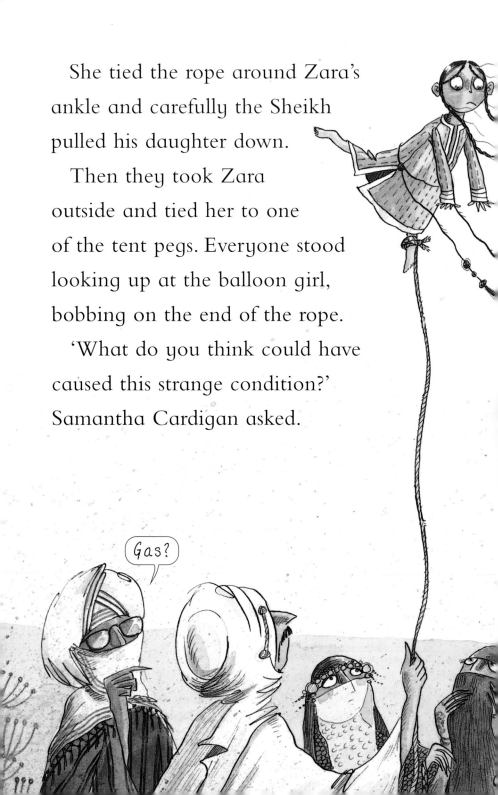

Gas?

The Sheikh shrugged and shook his head.

'Her mother thinks she may have swallowed soap bubbles. My brother thinks it must be that gas they put in balloons. No one knows.'

Rabbit tugged at Samantha Cardigan's sleeve and gave her a pleading look.

'I said no!' she told him sternly. 'You can just wait until dinner-time.'

Not now, rabbit!

I wish I could fly, too.

She turned back to the Sheikh.

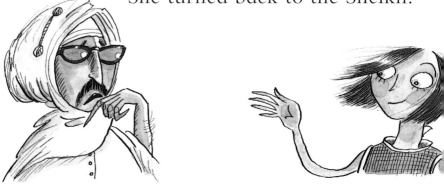

'I must apologise for my friend's lack of manners. He's only a rabbit, you see. But you know, I'll bet that genie we met this morning had something to do with this.'

The Sheikh went white with fear.

The Genie is all powerful!

'You met a genie this morning? May heaven preserve you. Tell me everything.'

Samantha Cardigan told him the story.

'You cannot imagine what danger you were in,' he said gravely. 'The Genie of the Sands is immensely powerful. He sleeps for years, but the slightest thing can wake him up! He will be very angry now.'

'But what about Zara? Do you think he's punishing her for something?' Samantha Cardigan asked.

Really?

The Sheikh looked sadder than ever.

'Not Zara . . . I am the one being punished. Once, many years ago, I was taking the goats to market. It was four days' journey and, on the way, I came upon the most beautiful oasis you can imagine. I had seventy goats with me and, of course, they rushed in to drink at the pond and eat the flowers.

How DARE you!

'Well, the Genie
of the Sands appeared,
as tall as a house and
furious that my animals
had fouled his private garden. For my
punishment, he declared that my best-loved
child would be stolen by the wind. Now
I fear his threat has come true!'

At War With the Wind

The Sheikh fell silent. Holding up one hand, he looked out over the dunes. Samantha Cardigan felt it as well — a puff of hot wind, as if someone had opened a huge oven door. Along the horizon, a vast red cloud was rolling towards them.

'Now he is coming,' the Sheikh announced solemnly. 'He rides on the wind.'

To the camels!

What's that?

The next thing she knew, people were
shouting and running every which way.
The women battened down the tents and
gathered up their goats and their children.
Zara's mother could not risk untying her
daughter, so she sat on the ground, clinging
to the rope.

Meanwhile, the men ran to fetch their swords, as if preparing for a great battle. Wrapping themselves in bright orange and yellow robes, they mounted their camels and horses and stood in long row, facing the wall of sand.

Budge up!

Running along behind the Sheikh, Samantha Cardigan cried, 'What are all the swords for? You can't fight the wind.'

'It is our tradition. One must never show the genie any weakness or fear. It is our desert too. We must be prepared to fight for it.'

Our honour is at stake.

Be careful!

With that, he leapt on to a beautiful
white horse and rode out to join the others.
Together they charged into the storm, waving
and slashing their curved swords. The genie's
face appeared in the cloud, laughing and
cursing and whooshing in circles.
With a puff of his breath,
he sent riders and
horses tumbling.

'I'm going to fight too,' Samantha Cardigan cried. 'I'm not afraid of that bully.'

Leaving her backpack by the tent, she grabbed a couple of sticks and passed one to Rabbit. Rabbit was not especially fond of fighting evil genies and she had to drag him by one arm.

Come on, Rabbit.

'You old windbag!' she shouted. 'We'll never let you take Zara.'

Hearing this, the genie became angrier than ever and he whirled around the two like a cyclone.

Faster and faster he flew, lifting them up off the ground. He carried them up and over the trees until they were directly above the pond.

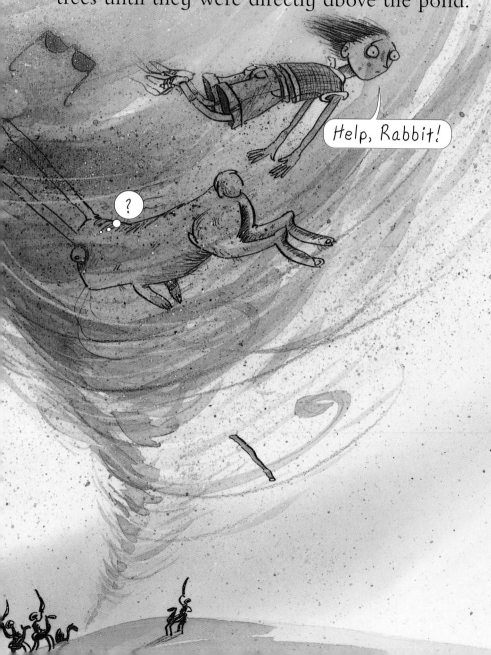

Then, all of a sudden, he laughed and flew away, letting them fall – **SPLASH!** – into the water.

Rabbits are not particularly strong swimmers, but luckily it wasn't very deep and they were able to wade out.

'We need a better plan,' Samantha Cardigan said, shaking the water from her shoes. 'Come on!'

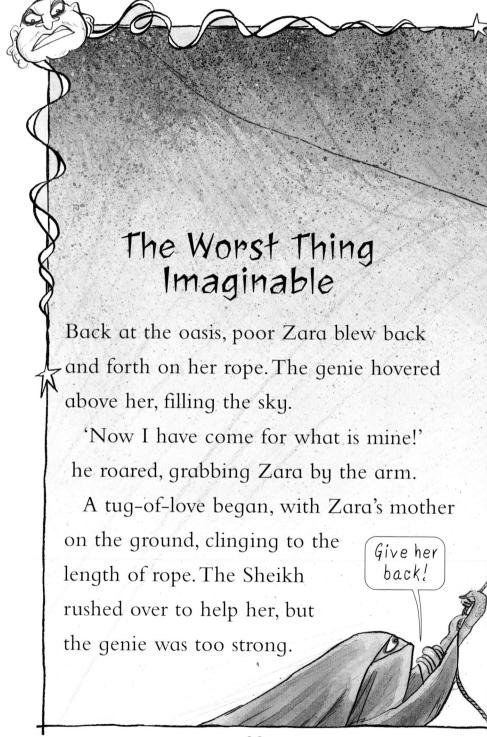

The Worst Thing Imaginable

Back at the oasis, poor Zara blew back and forth on her rope. The genie hovered above her, filling the sky.

'Now I have come for what is mine!' he roared, grabbing Zara by the arm.

A tug-of-love began, with Zara's mother on the ground, clinging to the length of rope. The Sheikh rushed over to help her, but the genie was too strong.

Give her back!

The rope began to slip through their
hands . . .

Samantha Cardigan and Rabbit dashed
back to where they had left her backpack.
Reaching inside, she pulled out a roll of
wallpaper, some paint and a pot of glue.

'Here, take the end of this,' she ordered.

Rabbit did his best to hold it flat while she wrote something in huge black letters. Then she slopped clear glue over the top of it.

Walking into a clearing, she shouted as loud as she could, 'Genie is a sissy pants!'

34

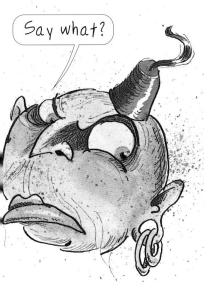

Say what?

The genie had not forgotten the scorpion sting. Now the horrid child was calling him names as well. He glared at her, holding Zara by one arm.

His moustache began to twitch. He went purple with rage.

Genie sucks a dummy and wears a nappy!

Then Samantha Cardigan and Rabbit unfolded their secret weapon.

On the piece of wallpaper, she had written the absolutely worst thing she could think of.

This he could not tolerate.

He let go of Zara.

The wind dropped to a whisper.

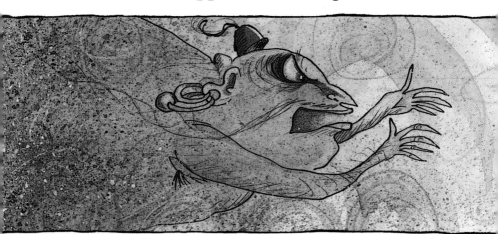

Bellowing like a bull with a sore head, he zoomed down, aiming directly for Samantha Cardigan. He reached out his massive hands, ready to grab her by the neck.

Tee hee!

But, at the last second, she and Rabbit jumped sideways.

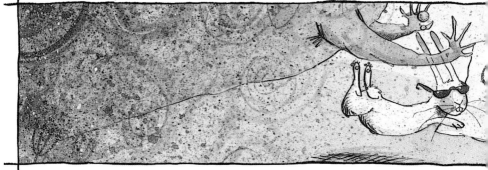

The genie slammed into the sticky paper and he stuck there.

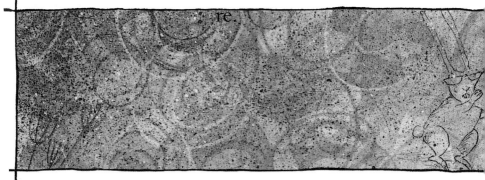

The great Genie of the Sands had become a giant sheet of sandpaper.

Got him!

Lettuce is Good For You

A great victory cry was heard for miles around and everyone congratulated Samantha Cardigan and Rabbit on their clever plan. Trapped on the sticky paper, the genie could do no more harm to anyone. But his final blast had brought so much sand with it that the tents were mostly buried. Zara was up to her armpits in sand. Everyone started digging, trying to recover their homes from the dunes.

Samantha Cardigan and Rabbit helped the Sheikh and his wife to free their daughter. All were greatly relieved to know that everything would soon be back to normal.

But, when the sand
was cleared away,
Zara was still floating
in the air! With
the genie defeated,
everyone naturally
assumed she would
come back down.
The Sheikh could
not believe his eyes.
He looked up at his
daughter, completely
at his wits' end.

Not again.

I don't believe it!

'The genie's revenge lives on, even after he is gone,' his wife cried. 'What's to become of my daughter? She'll have to live in a cage like a canary.'

The Sheikh tried to comfort her.

'Perhaps we could move to the city,' he suggested. 'She could get a job as a window cleaner.'

Zara began to cry. She didn't want to live in a birdcage or be a window cleaner. She wanted to chase the goats and play with her friends as she had always done.

My poor child!

Samantha Cardigan felt utterly miserable. Her plan had failed. She couldn't think of what to do or say. Rabbit tugged at her sleeve and whispered in her ear.

'Oh, for heaven's sake,' she cried. 'Yes, you can have a lettuce now, if you must!'

Reaching into her backpack, she thrust the lettuce at him.

Rabbit went to retrieve the inflatable ladder. He carried it over to where Zara was floating. He climbed up and started feeding her the lettuce. Samantha Cardigan groaned and looked away. What a dumb, rabbitty thing to do! As if eating lettuce was going to help anything.

But amazingly, Zara
began to come down.
By the time she had
finished the whole
lettuce, she was back
on the ground. She
untied the rope and
ran into her mother's arms.

The Sheikh exclaimed,
'But this is extraordinary.
How did he do that?'

Zara!
Thank
goodness!

Mummy!

Samantha Cardigan was equally astounded. Rabbit went over and whispered to her. She laughed and gave him a big hug.

'Did Zara eat a lot of chillies yesterday?' she asked.

You clever thing!

It was nothing.

'Why, yes . . . we had a very hot curry. Why do you ask?'

'Chillies make you hot inside. Heat rises. Because Zara is so little, it lifted her up off the ground. Eating that lettuce cooled her off, so she came back down. It never had anything to do with the genie.'

The Sheikh was so happy he did a special
dance that desert people do to say thank
you to the world. Zara's mother lit a fire
to prepare dinner.

'Not too much chilli!' Samantha Cardigan
and Zara called together. They laughed and
ran off with Rabbit to find the goats.